SOPHIE
the CIRCUS PRINCESS

by Stig Claesson • translated by Susanna Stevens • illustrated by Friso Henstra

SIMON & SCHUSTER
BOOKS FOR YOUNG READERS

SIMON & SCHUSTER BOOKS FOR YOUNG READERS
An imprint of Simon & Schuster Children's Publishing Division
1230 Avenue of the Americas, New York, New York 10020
This English translation copyright © 1995 by Susanna Marie Ferrell Stevens
Original Swedish text copyright © 1982 by Stig Claesson
Illustrations copyright © 1995 by Friso Henstra
All rights reserved including the right of reproduction
in whole or in part in any form.
SIMON & SCHUSTER BOOKS FOR YOUNG READERS
is a trademark of Simon & Schuster.
Book design by David Neuhaus
The text for this book is set in 14-point Zapf International Lite.
The illustrations were done in ink and watercolor.
Manufactured in the United States of America

10 9 8 7 6 5 4 3 2 1

Library of Congress Cataloging-in-Publication Data
Claesson, Stig. [Jag möter en cirkusprincessa. English]
Sophie the circus princess / by Stig Claesson ; translated by
Susanna Stevens ; illustrated by Friso Henstra.   p.   cm.
Summary: Sophie tells a young friend the sad story of why she
abandoned her career as a circus performer, but the story has an
unexpected happy ending. [1. Circus—Fiction.] I. Henstra, Friso, ill.
II. Title. PZ7.C5215So 1995 [E]—dc20 93-16780 CIP AC
ISBN: 0-671-87008-4

For Joanna, Ilona, and Michelle
—S.C.

For Gordon Stuart Ferrell
—S.S.

For Eveline
—F.H.

$\int$et far back from the side of a big road, near a forest, at the end of the world where the sun goes down, there was once upon a time a little cottage where a little old lady named Sophie lived, who dressed in black from head to toe.

Sometimes she would chop wood, and sometimes she would fetch water, and sometimes she would feed her nine hens. She also had a cow that hung about outside her house. When she had nothing to do, she would sit perfectly still on a rib-backed settee in her little kitchen.

My grandfather, the shoemaker, also lived in a house set far back from the side of the road, near the forest. When I was little, I used to sit with him in his workshop and watch him repair shoes. He was teaching me his trade because it was expected that someday I, like my father before me, would become a village cobbler.

But sometimes, when I could not keep my fingers off things and I poked through my grandfather's various tools, he would say to me: "Go visit lonely little old Sophie. Surely you can help her with something."

If little old Sophie had no work for me to do, we would sit on her settee drinking coffee. And then, sometimes, she would perform.

She would fetch a chair, and we would walk outside to her cow; and little old Sophie would set down the chair, climb up, and stand on the cow's back.

She could even balance just on one leg—on either her left one or her right. But Sophie could no longer turn somersaults on the cow's back.

Once she could. When she was young, she had left the old country and joined a circus troupe in America. Sophie had been the most beautiful horseback rider in the whole world, and audiences had stood up and cheered her splendid

performances. She could jump from the back of one running horse to another, and she could turn somersault after somersault. Now it was all she could do to stand on one leg on her scrawny cow.

One day, when we had returned to the settee in her kitchen after she had stood on her cow, I asked her why she had left the circus and come to live in this small house with her cow and nine hens.

She told me that one evening, as she was resting in her circus wagon after a performance, she heard a knock at the door and discovered a handsome young man outside in a striped suit and a strange-looking hat and a big mustache. He introduced himself as the prince of Pomerania. He presented her with flowers and said he wanted to marry her because she was such a graceful circus princess.

The prince of Pomerania was very handsome in his striped suit and his strange-looking hat and his mustache; and, besides that, he smoked fragrant tobacco in a curved pipe. Sophie had told herself that she could not imagine anything finer than being the princess of Pomerania.

So Sophie and the prince in the striped suit ran off to Chicago to get married, and afterward they stayed in a hotel room where they sat in matching chairs, holding hands.

They were very happy, until one day the police knocked at the door and carefully led away the prince—who turned out not to be a prince at all but an imposter.

It seemed that in the past few years he had assumed many different identities—among them a doge of Venice, a Romanian movie star, and a British stunt flier.

Then Sophie had to sit all alone in her hotel room because the prince was sent to a stone quarry to work for many a long year.

Sophie was very fond of the prince—even though he was not a prince at all—so she visited him at the hot stone quarry where he worked with all the other unfortunates. Then one day she told him that she forgave him but that she was going to return to her homeland to buy a little cottage and maybe a cow. And that is just what she did.

She told me she had been happy all the years since, chopping
wood, fetching water, feeding her hens, and standing on
her cow.

Then one day the prince appeared.

I was sitting on the steps outside my grandfather's house
when a horse and wagon drove up and out of the wagon
stepped a tall, handsome old gentleman in a striped suit and
an American hat, who smoked a curved pipe with fragrant
tobacco.

The moment I saw him I knew who he was: the false prince
of Pomerania.

He said something to me that I did not understand, but I took him by the hand and motioned him to follow me. He carried a strange bag inside of which I assumed were silk shirts and foreign coins.

We walked closer and closer to Sophie's cottage; and when we got near enough, we saw that Sophie, who must have known that he was coming, had dressed up in her old circus costume and stood waiting for him on the back of her astonished cow.

I stopped and watched as the prince continued walking proudly toward Sophie. Then I returned home to tell my grandfather that the prince had come to visit Sophie.

My grandfather listened in amazement. He removed his leather apron and combed his hair, and we walked down

toward Sophie's cottage. But there was nothing to see when we arrived other than the cow peacefully chewing its cud and smoke rising from Sophie's chimney.

"You must be telling the truth," exclaimed Grandfather. "There's a whiff of strange tobacco in the air."

Then Sophie appeared, still dressed as a circus princess, and invited us to come inside and meet the false prince—whom we found sitting on her rib-backed settee, smiling.

As we walked home later that day, my grandfather told me he was glad that little old Sophie would have someone with whom to share her later years.

Sophie and the false prince lived happily ever after. And whenever I visited, they sat side by side on the rib-backed settee—Sophie upright and perfectly still, and the prince reclining comfortably on the cushions—both with smiles on their faces and holding hands.

While Sophie chopped the wood, fetched the water, and fed the nine hens, the prince would stroll in the garden with his pipe in his smiling mouth, humming circus music. Only rarely now did Sophie stand on her cow.

Ever since the day the false prince appeared, I dreamed of owning a striped suit and a strange-looking hat and a suitcase filled with silk shirts and foreign coins. When I turned sixteen, I left the small village where my family lived and crossed the sea to America, where I became an artist. After struggling for some years, I became quite successful—and my paintings of circus performers in particular brought me honor and recognition.

And though I searched, I never found a circus performer as beautiful as little old Sophie. I can still see her performing just for me, standing on one leg on her cow, in front of her little cottage set far back from the side of the road, near the forest, at the end of the world where the sun goes down.